GOOD

ARE BETTER

BY LOUIS SLOBODKIN

THE VANGUARD PRESS

WITH
LOVE

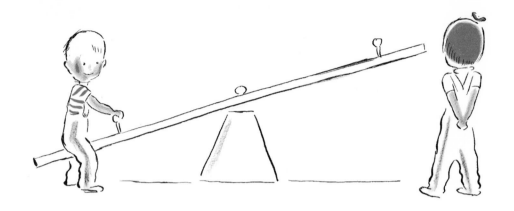

ONE IS GOOD,

BUT TWO ARE BETTER,

YOU NEED TWO PEOPLE

FOR A LETTER.

YOU CAN WRITE IT,

AND YOU CAN READ IT,

BUT USE A STAMP;

THE LETTER WILL NEED IT.

ONE PULLING A WAGON

IS NOT ENOUGH,

YOU NEED TWO

WHEN THE ROAD IS ROUGH.

YOU CAN PUSH,

AND YOU CAN PULL,

NOW LOAD THE WAGON

UNTIL IT'S FULL.

ONE CAN SWING

ALONE IN THE SUN,

BUT YOU NEED TWO

TO HAVE MORE FUN.

YOU CAN SING,

AND YOU CAN SWING

HIGH AS THE SKY

OR ANYTHING.

ONE IN A BOAT,

PLAYING DOWN AT THE SHORE,

CAN'T GO VERY FAR

WITH ONLY ONE OAR,

BUT IF THERE ARE TWO,

TWO OARS AND TWO FRIENDS,

YOU CAN ROW

'ROUND THE WORLD

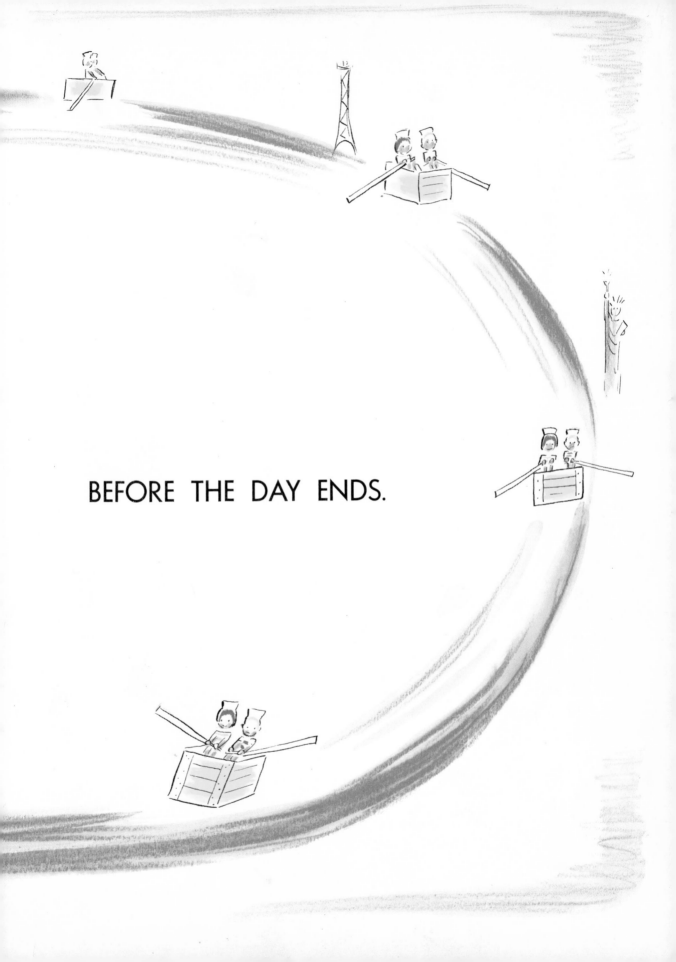

BEFORE THE DAY ENDS.

ONE PLAYING STORE,

SELLING BEANS AND RICE,

NEEDS SOMEONE TO BUY;

THAT MAKES IT NICE.

YOU CAN SELL

AND YOU CAN BUY,

THEN YOU CAN WRAP

AND YOU CAN TIE.

ONE WITH A BALL

NEEDS ONE WITH A BAT;

BASEBALL IS BETTER

PLAYED LIKE THAT.

YOU CAN BAT,

AND YOU CAN THROW,

HIT THE BALL

AND AWAY YOU GO.

ONE CAN RUN,

OR ONE CAN LAG,

BUT YOU NEED TWO

FOR PLAYING TAG.

YOU CAN RUN,

AND YOU CAN CHASE;

WHEN YOU ARE CAUGHT,

THEN RUN A RACE.

ONE MAY HIDE,

OR ONE MAY PEEK,

BUT YOU NEED TWO

FOR HIDE-AND-SEEK.

YOU CAN HIDE,

AND YOU CAN LOOK,

THEN ALL SIT DOWN

AND SHARE A BOOK.

YES, ONE IS GOOD,

BUT WHEN THERE ARE MORE,

SAY TWO OR THREE

OR MORE THAN FOUR,

YOU ALL CAN SING,

AND YOU ALL CAN PLAY,

AND YOU ALL CAN HAVE

A WONDERFUL DAY.